RECEIVED
2018

D0537037

NO LONGER PROPERTY OF
NO LONGER PROPERTY OF
SEATTLE PUBLIC LIBRARY

For my family:
Lori, Amelie & Madaline

Copyright © 2018 by Noah Klocek. All rights reserved. No part of this book may be reproduced, transmitted, or stored in an information retrieval system in any form or by any means, graphic, electronic, or mechanical, including photocopying, taping, and recording, without prior written permission from the publisher. First edition 2018. Library of Congress Catalog Card Number pending. ISBN 978-0-7636-9426-5. This book was typeset in Filosofia. The illustrations were created digitally.
Candlewick Press, 99 Dover Street, Somerville, Massachusetts 02144. visit us at www.candlewick.com.
Printed in Humen, Dongguan, China. 18 19 20 21 22 23 APS 10 9 8 7 6 5 4 3 2 1

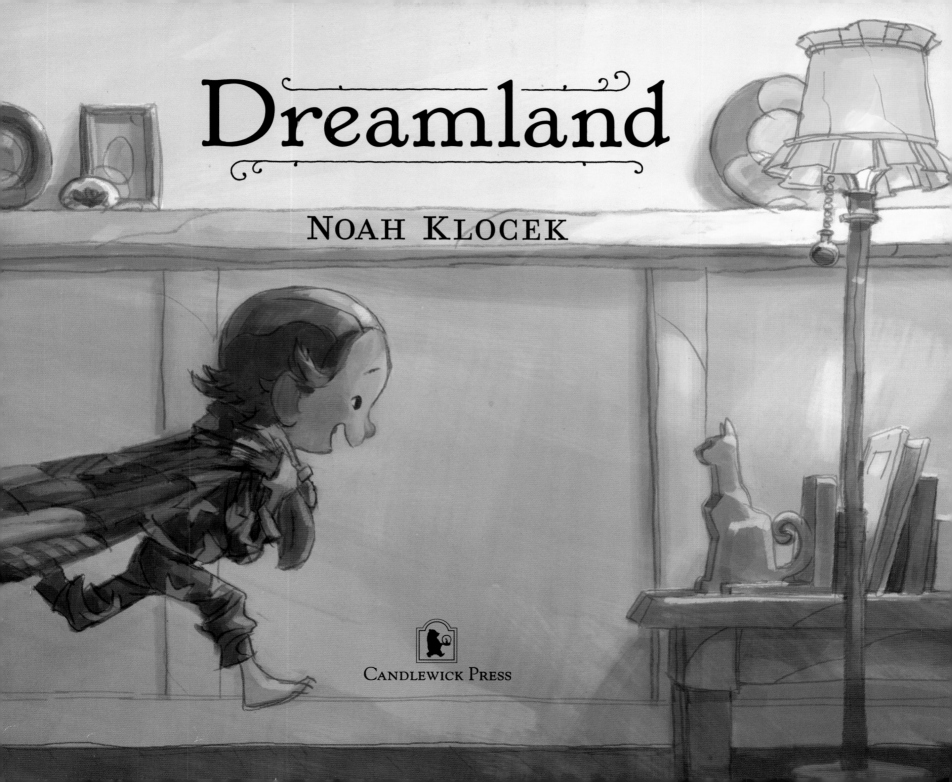

Dreamland

NOAH KLOCEK

CANDLEWICK PRESS

Amelie loved everything about bedtime.
She loved wrapping up in her favorite blanket.
She loved listening to bedtime stories.

More than anything, she loved to dream.

But her dreams
were often hard to find.

Most nights, Amelie had to
set out in search of them.

Along the way, she was slowed by
the cold she felt in her toes . . .

and the uncomfortable spots in the bed.

She struggled past the moonlight that fell in her room . . .

and waded through the blankets
that seemed lost in the sheets.

She marched by
the darkness in every corner . . .

and tamed all the shapes

that hid in the shadows.

She danced past the tick and tock
of the clock . . .

and traveled beyond the whistle of a distant train.

and far

She traveled high

and wide.

She traveled low

and deep

and dark.

Until somewhere in the night,
Amelie stumbled upon slumber . . .

and found herself in her favorite dreams.